# AND THE
# ROBOT WENT...

## Michelle Robinson
### Illustrated by Sergio Ruzzier

CLARION BOOKS

Houghton Mifflin Harcourt
Boston • New York

The Nosy Fox looked in the box,

and the Robot went . . .

# BOOOO.

The Nosy Fox looked
in the box,

the Eager Beaver pulled the lever,

and the Robot went . . .

The Nosy Fox looked in the box,

the Eager Beaver pulled the lever,

the Wicked Witch flicked the switch,

and the Robot went . . .

The Nosy Fox looked
in the box,

the Eager Beaver
pulled the lever,

the Wicked Witch
flicked the switch,

the Bear in a Blazer fired the laser,

and the Robot went . . .

The Nosy Fox looked
in the box,

the Eager Beaver
pulled the lever,

the Wicked Witch
flicked the switch,

the Bear in a Blazer
fired the laser,

the Crocodile turned the dial,

and the Robot went . . .

The Nosy Fox looked
in the box,

the Eager Beaver
pulled the lever,

the Wicked Witch
flicked the switch,

the Bear in a Blazer
fired the laser,

the Crocodile turned the dial,

the Blue Gnu
twisted the screw,

and the Robot went . . .

    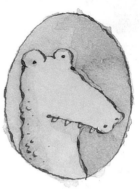

The Nosy Fox looked in the box, the Eager Beaver pulled the lever, the Wicked Witch flicked the switch, the Bear in a Blazer fired the laser, the Crocodile turned the dial,

the Band of Knights polished the lights,

the Blue Gnu twisted the screw,

and the Robot went . . .

 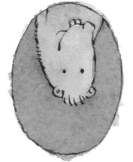 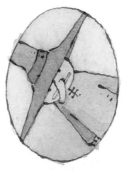  

The Nosy Fox looked in the box,

the Eager Beaver pulled the lever,

the Wicked Witch flicked the switch,

the Bear in a Blazer fired the laser,

the Crocodile turned the dial,

the Blue Gnu twisted the screw,

the Band of Knights polished the lights,

the King of Dogs clobbered the cogs,

and the Robot went . . .

Then along came **me.**

I found the key.

# Krank! Krrrank! Krrrrrrrrank!

*Now* let's try it.

Clobber the cogs, King of Dogs!

Polish the lights, Band of Knights!

Twist the screw, Blue Gnu!

Turn the dial, Crocodile!

Fire the laser, Bear in a Blazer!

Flick the switch, Wicked Witch!

Pull the lever, Eager Beaver!

Hide in the box, Nosy Fox!

THANK. YOU.

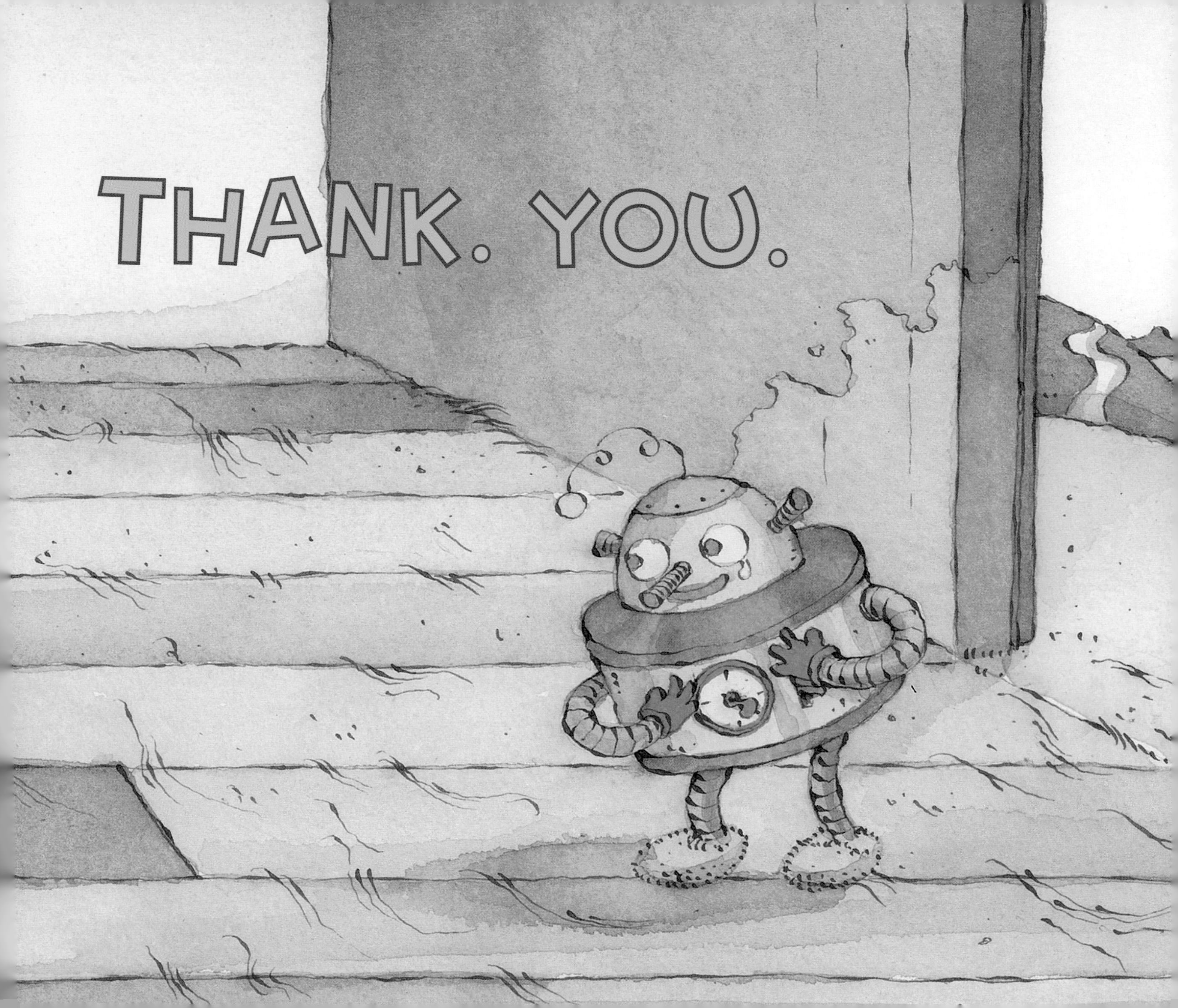

And the Robot . . .

. . . went.

For Ismene Catchpole—M.R.  •  For Ava—S.R.

Clarion Books  3 Park Avenue, New York, New York 10016   Text copyright © 2017 by Michelle Robinson    Illustrations copyright © 2017 by Sergio Ruzzier  All rights reserved.
For information about permission to reproduce selections from this book, write to trade.permissions@hmhco.com or to Permissions, Houghton Mifflin Harcourt Publishing Company,
3 Park Avenue, 19th Floor, New York, New York 10016. Clarion Books is an imprint of Houghton Mifflin Harcourt Publishing Company.  www.hmhco.com  The illustrations in this book were
done in pen and ink and watercolors on paper. The text was set in Bodoni Egyptian Pro. Library of Congress Cataloging-in-Publication Data is available. ISBN 978-0-544-58652-9
Manufactured in China    SCP 10 9 8 7 6 5 4 3 2 1   4500641782